COAT
ITALIAN
SALAMI
EYES EXAMINED
PARIS
CUT RATE
OPTICIANS
REPAIRING
WHILE U WAIT
SALE
LIVE
POULTRY
MARKET
LIVE FISH

Hurdy-Gurdy Holiday

Lithographs by Barbara Latham
Story by Leah Gale

HARPER & BROTHERS · *Publishers* · NEW YORK · LONDON

10—2
First Edition
K—R

Hurdy-Gurdy Holiday

From the distance came the droning sounds of Pietro's hand organ.

"Frisco's coming," screamed a young ragamuffin.

"The monkey! The monkey!" called many voices.

The tinny music drew children like a magnet. From all corners of the lower East Side street, they pushed toward the organ. They stopped whatever they were doing—crying or fighting or playing tag.

They crowded around the monkey—little children and big children, happy children and solemn children, dirty children and clean children.

Frisco, the monkey, knew many clever tricks. He brushed off his tiny red and blue cap and doubled forward in a bow. Then, leaping to a window sill of an old tenement, he hopped and somersaulted in his funny monkey way.

"He lik-a da good music," Pietro often said. "Then he dance."

Frisco was a very special monkey even if he did scratch you when he didn't like you.

Frisco's full name was Francisco Puccini Della Maria Santonelli.

"Such a big name for such a small monkey," people would say.

"He havva da bigga tail," Pietro would answer. "Yes? No?"

It was Miss Walker, the school teacher, who said he looked like a tail tacked on to a monkey.

Flip! Frisco caught a penny in his little cap and blinked up at the open window. Flip! He caught another. Frisco tipped his cap to the window gallery and clumsily clapped his hands. Then he frisked down the rusty metal railing with his tail curled upward like a question mark.

"Such a funny face!" crowed a tiny boy.

"Wish I hadda penny," whispered a little girl.

"What a pretty red jacket!" exclaimed her older sister.

There was no doubt that Frisco's jacket, trimmed with gold, looked very grand with the purple velvet trousers. Pietro knew what a well-dressed monkey should wear.

Frisco bowed and the crowd laughed, but no one gave Frisco any more money.

Pietro stopped grinding and tugged Frisco's chain.

No more business!

With a leap and a hop, Frisco found his way to Pietro's shoulder. His sad, wise face peered about at the children.

Frisco tipped his tiny cap two times—three times. Then off they went.

Dark-eyed Tony stared thoughtfully after them. Tony was a boy of ten, and he was lonely. Tony had a plan. He wanted Frisco for himself—just for a little while.

And so, humming a little nervously to himself, he scuffed along behind Pietro.

When Pietro stopped for a hot dog at Frederico's pushcart, Tony stopped too. He pretended to inspect a tower of cans in a store window.

"It-sa fin-a day," he heard Pietro say to Frederico between big bites.

"Just-a right!" said Frederico. "How-sa monkey business?"

"Not-a so good," said Pietro.

Frisco climbed down to the sunny side of Frederico's cart and blinked at the crowds.

The people on First Avenue were going about their business. The peddlers at the pushcarts along the sidewalks were shouting out prices; the housewives who passed were examining the bargains.

Nobody noticed Frisco—nobody but Tony.

Suddenly Tony dashed up to the cart. Quick as a flash he unchained Frisco. Grabbing the startled monkey, he zig-zagged through the crowds.

"Ee-ee-ee!" squealed Frisco.

"Fermatelo!" shouted Pietro in Italian.

"Ostanovite yevo!" shouted a woman in Russian.

"Khop im!" shouted a woman in Yiddish.

In English all they meant was "Stop him!"

But nobody did.

Pietro lumbered and puffed along the sidewalk in the direction in which Tony had disappeared with Frisco.

"A leetle monkey with a bigga tail?" he gasped to passersby. "A leetle monkey? A bigga tail?"

"He went this-a way." A woman pointed.

"He went that-a way." A man pointed.

1ST AVE
E. 11 ST.

Pietro went "this-a" way and "that-a" way, but he couldn't find his monkey.

Only Tony knew what had become of the frisky little fellow with the sad face and merry ways.

That morning business was going on as usual in Guido's sausage shop.

A woman was complaining about the prices.

Her little daughter was watching a spotted dog daydreaming at the end of a leash.

Near the doorway, a skimpy black cat squinted at the bustle of First Avenue.

The store was alive with garlic and strong cheeses, and dark with the sausages that hung from the ceiling.

There was a forest of them—clusters of yellow sausages like grapes and long brown sausages like punching bags, shriveled sausages and sausages shaped like bottles, straight sausages and hooped ones.

Suddenly Tony, with Frisco high on his shoulder, appeared in the doorway.

"Ma-a! Ma-a!" wailed the little girl, taking no chances out in the open. She tugged her mother's skirt.

"Wuff-wuff," barked the dog, straining at the leash. "Wuff-wuff."

"S-s-s-s-s," hissed the cat, stiffening his back and tail for battle.

Chattering with terror, Frisco gave Tony a quick scratch on his arm.

"Ouch!" shouted Tony, loosening his hold on the monkey.

With a hop from Tony's head to the counter, Frisco was free.

The pyramids of food began to topple. Down tumbled the golden cans of olive oil, the long crisp bread sticks, the round red cheeses. They rolled and clattered and bumped to the floor.

Frisco scrambled up on a long hanging sausage and swung back and forth by his tail.

"Quiet, Caruso! Quiet!" shouted the dog's stout mistress.

The face of the pudgy storekeeper grew red with anger. "Stoppa da racket!" he thundered. "Getta da zoo outa my store!"

The lady with the dog strutted out of the sausage shop, jerking the leash.

The little girl's mother, in her rush to follow, tripped over the cat, which began to yowl.

"Keep your sausages!" exclaimed a cranky old lady, who had been hit on the head by a cheese. She hurried out of the store.

Frisco swung back and forth like a pendulum. Back and forth ran the storekeeper. Then with a leap Frisco was out the back window along with the sausage.

"You bandeet!" shouted the storekeeper, chasing after Tony with a baloney. Out of the store darted Tony, with the storekeeper at his heels. Behind the storekeeper puffed the storekeeper's wife.

ED

Down Eleventh Street, up Tenth Street, down Ninth Street they dodged. Then Tony shot around a corner and was swallowed by the crowd.

It was at that moment that Pietro lumbered into the sausage shop.

"A leetle monkey? A bigga tail?" he gasped to the sausages.

There was no answer.

One look at the topsy-turvy store and Pietro was happy. Frisco couldn't be far away.

"Frisco! Frisco!" he called.

Still no answer.

Pietro rushed out into the street. He stopped people who were passing to ask if they had seen his Frisco.

"He went this-a way," a woman pointed.

"He went that-a way," a man pointed.

Pietro went "this-a" way and "that-a" way, but he couldn't find his monkey.

What had become of Frisco?

What, indeed!

Dragging the sausage, Frisco scampered out into the long narrow alley behind the store.

"Woff-woff," barked an ill-bred dog, sniffing the pleasant sausage smell.

"Wiff-wiff," barked another.

"Wouff-wouff," barked a third.

Dogs closed in on Frisco from hidden corners of the alley—big dogs and little dogs, lean dogs and fat ones.

Soon a lot of dogs were chasing Frisco! Up over the fence he clambered, dropping the sausage.

There in front of him was a dark canyon formed by two high walls of windows. A jungle of fire-escapes cluttered with wet mops and pails and bedding zig-zagged up the buildings.

All the way up the block, there was a procession of wash waving like flags on the lines. There were red and yellow and blue dresses, sparkling white sheets and sheets that were grayish. There was the family underwear lined up according to size, shirts and stockings that were torn and those neatly mended.

Frisco shot up to a fifth-story fire-escape and buried himself in a basket of wet clothes.

It was Mrs. Rosen's basket. The basket was very full, for Mrs. Rosen had a family of eight.

"Sammy, Sammy," called Mrs. Rosen, looking down into the backyard. "He's a smart boy in school, my Sammy, God bless him," she said across to Mrs. Murphy. "But he's never around to go to the store."

Mrs. Rosen sighed. "Prices are going sky high, Mrs. Murphy."

Without looking, Mrs. Rosen picked out poor Frisco's tail from the basket and was about to hang Frisco on the line.

"Oi, a cat!" she screamed, dropping him quickly.

Screeching, Frisco swung himself to the roof top.

"Malpeh!" screamed Mrs. Rosen in Yiddish.

"Una scimmia!" screamed Mrs. Giovanni in Italian.

"Obezyana!" screamed Mrs. Nevsky in Russian.

In English they meant "Monkey!"

Further up the block a window was wide open in Mrs. Plachek's kitchen. The bedding was airing on the fire-escape while Mrs. Plachek was out shopping.

Frisco paused to sniff the geraniums in Mrs. Plachek's flowerpot garden on the window ledge. He picked one to wear, but when the stem wouldn't go through his buttonhole he tossed it aside.

Then he hopped down through the open window into the kitchen.

There he made himself right at home.

There was a kettle of water singing merrily away on the back of the stove. Frisco climbed up to investigate it. He started to pick up the hot kettle, but dropped it quickly, barely missing his toes. Fortunately he didn't spill any of the hot water on himself.

He inspected the china cupboard and broke five of Mrs. Plachek's best cups and saucers.

On the table was a birthday present for Mrs. Plachek's grandson. It was a sugary white lamb, bedecked with pink roses and blue satin bows, all neatly resting in a frilly lace-paper doily. A little flag waved proudly over the cake. As soon as Frisco saw the flag he stuck it in his hat.

At that Mrs. Plachek's canary began to scold. Startled, Frisco turned quickly. His tail swished the whole beautiful confection to the floor!

He hopped down to sample the crumbs and frosting. When a key

SUN SHIN
MALT

squeaked in the lock, he was back up on the table nibbling at the three cakes still there. He bounded into the broom closet.

He tore open a pillow on one of the chairs. Flurries of feathers floated up into the air and slowly settled like a blanket of new-fallen snow over tables and chairs. They got into Frisco's eyes and tickled his nose.

Through the doorway walked Mrs. Plachek. "Oh!" she exclaimed when she saw the feather blizzard.

"Mice!" Her alarmed eyes caught sight of the nibbled cakes on the table. "Oh dear, dear," and she almost wept at the sight of the crumbled birthday present. Sadly she reached for the broom.

But it wasn't the broom handle she picked out of the closet; it was a tail with a squealing monkey at the other end.

Up on a chair hopped Mrs. Plachek.

Down to the floor plopped Frisco.

That unlucky tail!

Trembling, Frisco scurried out the door and into the long dark hallway. The floor there had just been scrubbed. It was still wet and somewhat soapy.

Poor Frisco lost his footing and slithered and skidded every which way, until he banged up against the door at Apartment 3 D.

Inside the kitchen living room, Mrs. Piazza was busily ironing with her back to the door.

Though the window was wide open, there was no driving out the mustiness from the walls, the damp odor of the clothes, and the general sour smell.

There were children of assorted sizes all about the room.

A little boy in his underclothing was running about clapping two pot covers together.

A tiny child was creeping under the sink after a cockroach.

A seven-year-old girl was making a doll out of a clothespin.

Everything seemed to be on the floor.

"Come in, come in, Mrs. Horn," called Mrs. Piazza when she heard the banging at the door. "It's open."

Just then Frisco pushed and the door opened.

Never had Mrs. Horn created such an impression!

"A monkey! A monkey!" shouted one of the children.

"You shouldn't talk that way to Mrs. Horn!" said Mrs. Piazza, hastily setting down the iron and turning around.

"My!" she gasped, when she saw her strange visitor.

The boy in his underwear and the girl with the clothespin began to chase after Frisco.

The baby under the sink settled down to a good cry.

All the other children crowded into a corner with big eyes and open mouths.

Frisco darted from the pile of wash to the ironing board, from the stack of dirty dishes to the chandelier, from the table to the bed.

One of the children grabbed a pot from the floor and pulled it over Frisco's head. Even Mrs. Piazza had to laugh, though she'd almost forgotten how. The girl with the clothespin caught hold of Frisco's tail, but she laughed so hard that she forgot to hold on.

Mrs. Cohen, who was spending part of the day helping out Mrs. Piazza, appeared in the bedroom doorway.

"Did I heard something?" she tried to say above the uproar.

All she saw of Frisco was his tail disappearing through the door.

No! Mrs. Horn had never created such an impression!

Frisco scampered out into the dark and dirty hall. It was filled with odors of a league of nations: the smell of Italian cheese, of Russian "Kapusta," of Hungarian goulash. There was a clattering noise as the pot bounced along the steps.

Down the banisters slid Frisco and out on to the crowded sidewalk.

TOYS AND NOVELTIES
98
ABC
GAME
5
19
10

Halfway down the block Frisco took shelter in a narrow doorway. Nobody appeared to notice him there, so he had time to catch his breath, straighten his coat, and tip his hat to just the right angle.

After a while, Frisco looked cautiously about—he was in front of a toy shop.

He tried out a rocking chair, but left that for a tricycle. He had never been on one before and pinched his toes trying to work the pedals.

The rocking horse interested him, but the teddy bear riding it squeaked too loud when Frisco started to take him off, so he had to give that up.

It was while Frisco was trying to untangle his tail from the elephant's trunk that he was discovered.

Shouted the storekeeper: "A monkey! You get right out of this . . ." But Frisco had already leaped.

His tail made it to a doll carriage suspended from a hook high on the wall. He pulled the rest of himself up after it.

But the storekeeper was right after poor Frisco. With a long pole he dislodged the carriage.

Frisco made himself into a ball when he saw what was coming, and rolled straight out of sight.

While Frisco scampered down Eighth Street, trailed by a laughing mob, Pietro was struggling along Tenth Street; while Frisco scampered on Tenth Street, Pietro was struggling along Eighth Street.

Poor Pietro! He was all out of breath. The hurdy-gurdy on his back felt like a fair-sized barn.

He dragged himself up a fire-escape and peeked in through an open window.

"A leetle monkey? A bigga tail?" he pleaded breathlessly.

"Help! Police! Police!" screamed the old lady inside.

Pietro clattered down the fire-escape—fearfully, but with a new idea. If the police didn't arrest him, maybe they would help him!

Meanwhile the throngs on Tenth Street swarmed around the unattached monkey. The rattling of boxes to the sidewalks and the rat-tat-tat of riveting had stopped. Automobiles honked and honked their horns, trying to get through the crowds.

Frisco perched on a sandwich man's sign and looked around him. Then he clambered over the cars and into the up-to-date market across the street. People inside were too busy shopping to notice the tiny monkey that darted up to the silver pipes below the ceiling.

Frisco hugged himself with terror. Between the long lines of colorful stands below him was a moving carpet of heads and hats and bundles.

The air was a mixture of many tempting odors—the smell of dill pickles, of fresh sea food, of sharp cheeses—the smell of sweet oranges, of moist greens, of raw meat.

Now and then excited voices could be heard above the general hubbub.

"Hey, two cents—oranges, two cents."

"Yes, sir, a bargain to you. Six cents."

"Graborannan you anee," shouted someone in a language all his own.

A peddler behind a vegetable stand was just about to weigh two pounds of potatoes. An old lady with a shawl around her head stood ready with the money in her hand.

Suddenly there was a squealing and a clatter. Frisco bounced into the scale.

"A potato?" exclaimed the startled woman, watching the scale dance.

All over the market, people pushed and stretched to see what had happened. One or two men made a grab for Frisco's moving tail.

There was a shower of potatoes and oranges as Frisco tried to cover his retreat. He hopped from stand to stand: from the stands loaded with crockery to the stands of slippery snails, from the stands with candy to the stocking stands, from the stands with pink "lox" and glittering white fish, to the stands of glistening olives.

Piles of food began to slide downhill; glass crashed to the floor.

Then Frisco was gone.

Just outside the market, a woman stopped to look into her shopping bag. She saw what looked like a red knob on a cap and was just about to take hold of it when out popped a pale, smooth monkey face.

It was Frisco!

With a spring from the woman's arm, Frisco was up on the pillar of the El. The woman dropped her shopping bag and ran.

Quick as a flash, Frisco swung himself up to the top of the steel skeleton. Then he frisked along the ties of the track as fast as his arms and legs could carry him.

People leaned out of third-story windows almost close enough to touch him.

Mrs. Villarsky saw him out of the corner of her eye and thought he was a paper bag blowing along.

"It must be windy outside," she said.

Soon the El began to shake and quiver under Frisco. A Third Avenue Express was roaring up along the track. The metal monster was growing bigger and noisier. Closer and closer it came—grinding, rattling, rumbling.

"Ee-ee-ee-ee," squealed Frisco, lowering himself to the pillar just in time to save his tail. With a few slides and leaps, he dropped to the street.

Frisco didn't seem to belong anywhere.

By this time Pietro had notified the police of the loss of his "leetle" monkey. The police wires began to buzz with complaints from all over the East Side.

The white-and-green police cars like smooth shiny beetles nosed through the streets hunting the monkey. Radio reports of his zig-zagging course came through from time to time.

"Calling Car 34 . . . Car 34 . . . Calling Car 45 . . . Car 45," blared the radios. "Monkey last seen on Fourth Street. Traffic jam."

Frisco had crossed against the lights.

A big red bus had screeched to a stop almost on top of him. The people inside were thrown on their noses.

The car behind had screeched its brakes and bumped into the bus.

Then the car behind the car behind the bus had screeched its brakes and bumped the car behind the bus.

The screeching and the bumping had spread to the whole long line of cars.

Frisco had clambered up to the top of the bus and taken a free ride.

"Calling Car 34 . . . Car 34. Calling Car 45 . . . Car 45. Monkey last seen at the Tompkins Square Playground."

There Frisco had slid from the chute till he wore out the seat of his trousers. Even Jimmy, the bully, didn't stand a chance for a slide.

Frisco made himself boss of the jungle gym and pushed the children off the bars.

PEPSI-COLA
7UP

He had capered and somersaulted on the swing till the counsellor discovered him.

"Of all things! No monkeys allowed," said she angrily, yanking him off by the tail.

"Last seen on Avenue A . . ."

"Last seen on Avenue B . . ."

"Last seen on Avenue C . . ."

Frisco seemed to be leading the police through the alphabet.

"Last seen on top of a picket sign on Bleecker Street . . ."

"Last seen at the Gouverneur Hospital . . ."

There Frisco had raced through the wards, making the lines on the temperature charts shoot up and down.

"It's against the rules," said the head nurse when she saw him.

The orderlies and the nurses and the doctors had chased him over beds and bottles out into the street.

By that time Frisco had grown very tired. He had hopped a ride on an old baby carriage a junkman was pulling. He rode there unnoticed for some time, but finally was chased again.

Then Frisco had disappeared.

He had fallen asleep behind a rubbish pile on an old fire-escape.

The windows of the East Side became pink from the rosy, dusty sunset. In the tenements, on the sidewalks, in the store windows, lights flashed on to stop the advance of the darkness.

The houses seemed to empty most of their tenants onto the stoops. The grocer with his apron big in front of him was sitting on a box outside the store. A group of the bigger boys were slouched against the candy-store window, jeering at passersby. Everywhere there were children who should have been in bed. They shouted, they pushed, they raced, they wrestled.

From a tenement window above a boarded-up store came the painful scraping of a violin. Gilbert Rosenthall was practicing.

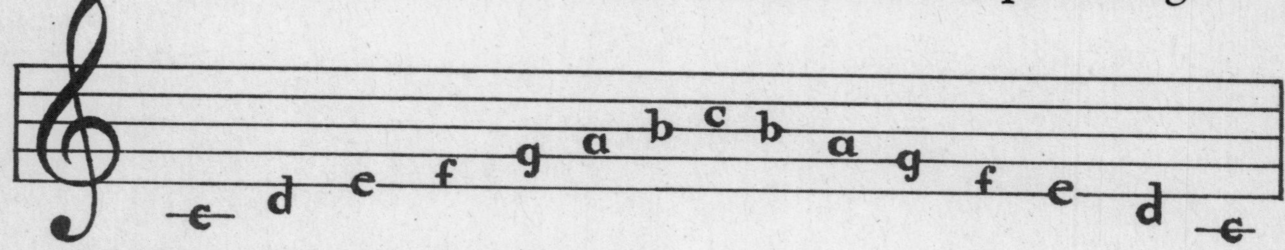

Up and down the scales he went.

People shivered and clapped their hands over their ears. In the gutter, a man selling "knishes" and an old woman pushing a rickety baby carriage piled high with junk hurried to make their escape.

"Listen to Mischa Elman," said Mrs. Holtz to Mrs. Goldberg, with a glance up at Gilbert's window.

Suddenly someone spied a small dark body darting along a fire-escape. It anchored itself by its long tail and swung to a lower level.

From the fourth-story fire-escape to the third, to the second, to the first, darted the monkey. Out from between the bars of the bottom one he peered about, curling his tail like a question mark. Then with a leap and a hop, he reached the sill of Gilbert's window.

There, to the shrill scratching of the fiddle, the monkey somersaulted expertly, clapped his hands, and bounced up and down.

"Una scimmia!" shouted an Italian woman.

"Obezyana!" shouted a Russian woman.

"Malpeh!" shouted a Jewish woman.

What they said, if you remember, was "Monkey!"

"He's dancing!" shouted a happy child's voice.

"It's Frisco!" shouted another.

And a tattered Frisco it was! There was much more monkey showing than there had been in the morning.

Windows on all sides were noisily flung higher.

On the street corner, a crowd that had gathered to listen to a speaker began to push toward the monkey.

" . . . the housing conditions on the East Side . . ." boomed out the speaker to fewer and fewer ears.

The people on the stoops, the children on the sidewalks, the grocer, the bigger boys, crowded about Frisco. Chin Lee took time off from his shirts to peek out the doorway.

Flip! Frisco caught the penny from a second-story window. He

tipped his cap to the window gallery and clumsily clapped his hands. Down dropped another. Flip! The pennies began to fly at Frisco till his pockets were full.

It was on Gilbert's window sill that a police car found him.

"There's the missing monkey," shouted Patrolman Kelly.

"He's sure caused enough trouble," said Jim O'Sullivan, the officer with him. "A man would be jailed for less:

"Breaking into homes,

"Wrecking stores,

"Causing traffic jams,

"Assaulting children in the playground,

"Exciting the patients at the hospital.

"We've got to catch him."

The crowd parted to make way for the two policemen.

"Break it up . . . break it up," shouted Kelly to the people.

"Who's going to bag him?" asked a tall boy, laughing.

"Frisco! Frisco!" called a voice. There was Pietro pushing forward in the crowd.

"My monkey!" he explained to Kelly. "My monkey!"

"Take him," said Kelly. "And hold on to him."

Gilbert's fiddle was still scratching up and down the scales.

Pietro laughed with joy to see Frisco hopping on the window sill.

"You see? He lika da good music," said he.

No one noticed a dark-eyed boy of ten who had arrived on the fringe of the mob. Everyone watched Frisco jump into Pietro's arms. Tony breathed a sigh of relief. He was through with Frisco and taking things that didn't belong to him.

Frisco, hopping to Pietro's shoulder, tipped his cap to the crowd.

Then as Frisco and Pietro started for home, old men and old women, big children and little children—on the sidewalks, on the stoops, at the windows—waved hats, hands, and handkerchiefs.

That in any language means "Good-by."